A Jewel of Hope

Second Edition

A Jewel of Hope   By Brie Nicole

I dedicate this book to all of the people that inspired me to write this story.

-Brie Nicole

Chapter 1

We all know the ancient stories of Merlin and Morgan Le Fay from the King Arthur story. Or even a more modern one like Harry Potter. But, do we really know their stories? Well I am certainly not going to give a history lesson about them. Today I'm going to tell you a different kind of story. The story of Claire Johnson, an amazingly average, typical 12 year old girl, that is until now.

"Dolphins are highly intelligent and are part of a toothed group of Orcas and Pilot whales". "Their diet includes fish, squid, and crustaceans. This information is for dolphins in general since there are many different species of dolphin in the world." said Claire as she was finishing her oral report. "Serena, you next" said Mrs. Marley the English teacher with pride. Why does Serena have to be the most popular girl in school, and all of my teachers' favorite student? Claire thought to herself.

Serena was a tall girl with straight, brown hair who needed everyone's attention. How she got their attention was different every day. It could be clothes, shoes, accessories, hairstyles, or anything like that. There was always a crowd following her, everywhere. "Polar bears are among the largest carnivores on earth, they exclusively eat Ringed Seals". Polar Bear cubs stay with their mothers for at least 2 1/2 years before they move out of the Den." said Serena "Aren't polar bears just so cute and interesting?" Serena asked with a slight smirk on her face. "That was so beautiful Serena; kids, take notes on Serena's gestures, calmness, and tone of voice." Mrs. Marley added. Mrs. Marley was short, wore glasses, and always tried to look young. (Serena helped; well, you can't blame her for trying) "Serena, how did you know polar bears were my favorite animal?" "A lucky guess" said Serena, glaring at Claire while walking back to her seat.

The feud between Claire and Serena all started in the 2nd grade when Claire moved into the town with her aunt and uncle. Serena hated her from the very beginning, glaring and really, just leaving her out, but the worst part was when Serena took Claire's best and only friend Allison. After that, Claire learned how to react to the many ways of Serena Winchester. As everyone did as they were told, Claire sat there and thought of what she would do that evening. Then the bell rang for lunch. "Why weren't you writing down notes like everybody else?" Serena asked Claire in the middle of the hallway. "Everyone knows that the only reason the class wrote those note is because they're afraid that Mrs. Marley would do something to them."

Serena, thinking out loud said "Or it could be because of my greatness, beauty, and popularity." While whispering Claire answered back "I highly doubt that" And went on her way to the lunch room, leaving Serena speechless." I think I handled that pretty well, thought Claire as she looked back at a jaw-dropped Serena. Serena was someone you would expect to start the gossip around the school. Of course, she started gossip about Claire. "Can you believe it?" She started "Claire said that I wasn't beautiful and popular and great." Serena finished. Which made the people sitting at the lunch table next to her gasp and stare at Claire who was sitting at the farthest table at the back of the lunchroom. Unsurprisingly, by herself. Claire dealt with this kind of stuff every day, so it didn't bother her. The bell rang for lunch to be over and everyone could hear it in the gloomy lighted, blue floored cafeteria. Surprisingly, you could hear it over Serena and her group plus the boys on the other side of the room gushing over Serena. About how cute she was, how popular she was, and who out of the boys would take her to the annual school dance. Finally everyone went out to study hall. Nope, no more recess for 6th graders.

Nothing was different in Study Hall, popular girls sit at one table, popular boys sit at another table, nerds sit in the front, and in the back of the room at yet another table was Claire, again all by herself. You might think study hall is a quiet and peaceful place to do work, but you would be wrong. The groups were continuing their conversations from lunch, and Claire was in fact doing her Geography extra credit. Claire did extra credit whenever she could, without being considered a nerd. Though her folks did not care much for Claire's grades, Claire thought it was important for the future. On the other hand, Science was next for Claire and Serena, so Claire got ready as Serena jabbered on with the popular girls about clothes and trends. "Ring", "Ring", "Ring", the bell sounded, as everyone scattered to their classes. Now on to Science class, thought Claire. "Welcome class" said Mrs. Jackson as the last of people entered. "Today we will be starting chapter 4." "This chapter is on energy." Started Mrs. Jackson.... Mrs. Jackson really gets into events, holidays, and of course science..... "First off class, you should know that the definition of energy is the ability to cause change." Serena suddenly raised her hand, which was odd for her considering she didn't like school.

"Yes, Serena"? Asked Mrs. Jackson "So if energy is the ability to cause change, does that mean that every time I change my make-up, hair, or clothes; that's energy?" That's not a bad comprehension for Serena, being Serena, Claire thought. "Well not exactly, but you have the idea." "Every time you breathe, put on make-up, change clothes or hairstyles, you're moving at least one part of your body, yes? So every time you move a finger, muscle, eyeball, or any other part of your body you are using energy, understand?" Like I said, she really gets into the spirit of science "Moving along, another thing you should know is that energy is measured in joules."

"Gasp!" yelled Erica, a part of Serena's popular clique. "Maybe if I go on daily walks and run more often I could gain a lot of jewels! I'll be rich!" "Not jewels as in crystals, joules as in the measurement of energy." Explained Mrs. Jackson "oh" said Erica in disappointment, meanwhile Mrs. Jackson was at her desk finishing up grading last minute papers. Mrs. Jackson finished just as the bell rang yet again. Finally, the last class of the day came! This class, Claire didn't care much for, so she listened but also daydreamed at the same time. Nobody paid any attention to her so it was super easy to daydream, even if it didn't look like she was doing it. Thoughts rushed through Claire's head as she walked into the beach scented room. The teacher for this class was a germaphobe, so she sprayed chemicals around the room to kill the germs, luckily they were scented, and unluckily this class was computer class. "Everyone, grab a Clorox wipe on your way in, and wipe down your computer." Said Ms. Grace and everyone did as they were told. "Get on the typing website" Added Ms. Grace. After about 45 minutes of typing the bell finally rang. Everyone rushed to their lockers to get their bags and other stuff and walked quickly out of the building.

While everyone was walking in their groups Claire stood alone, and even though it had been exactly 3 hours from lunch, the conversations continued. You could still hear Serena's group talking about trends, the nerds talking about the bones in the human body, and still the popular boys gushing and arguing. "Everyone in Mrs. Jackson's class please report to her room before you leave." Said the office, over the intercom. Right then everyone turned around and went straight to Mrs. Jackson's room.

"Sorry everyone, I know you were heading home for your winter break but I forgot to tell you about your project due January 10th." "I will pair you up." "Serena and Erica, Jackie and Allison, Lilly and Macy, Zac and Luke, Dylan and Ethan, Cole and Alex." (exc.) nobody paired up with Claire. "Your projects need to be about what you think is wrong with the world today." And with that everyone went out of the room and rode or walked home.

When Claire got home, Myra was there waiting for her. What a delight. Claire thought with much sarcasm. "How was school?" Myra asked. "Okay, I guess." Claire answered. "Well that's nice, but don't think it's going to get any better." Myra declared. "Why?" Claire asked "Don't you remember, you are supposed to do my homework? Get in the kitchen and start on my homework." Myra demanded! Claire silently did as she was told and started on Myra's and her own homework.

After homework Claire decided to go to her room. Claire's room was not what you would expect to see in a mansion. Her room was a piece of the basement with a trampoline implanted into the ground and an old fashioned closet near to the door to exit and enter Claire's room. A pile of blankets filled one corner as the trampoline bed filled the other and the armoire filled the third, left with bells in the fourth corner so that Claire's aunt, uncle, and cousin, Myra, could contact her, like in Disney's cartoon Cinderella. Unlike Myra's room with more toys and clothes than you could ever imagine. It was huge! Claire on the other hand was jumping on her bed thinking about what she should cook for dinner. Claire's aunt always loved to cook, but tonight her and Claire's uncle were going out for dinner because every month they say that Myra and Claire should have some quality time together.

Claire honestly thought that they either just wanted to get away from bossy Myra or shy, quiet Claire. Claire decided on baked chicken and went upstairs to start making it. Then Myra stormed in. "Did you do my homework?" Myra asked as she sat down to start eating. "Yes." Answered Claire as she served the food. After a few minutes of silence and noises of Myra's sloppy eating "So what are you going to do after dinner?" Asked Claire. "I will be texting and calling my friends in my room, so don't bother me." "Okay." Answered Claire "I'll mind my own business". And with that, they went their separate ways. While Myra texted and called in her room, Claire went outside and decided to adventure into the woods behind her relatives' house. Suddenly, a brightly blue colored butterfly startled her. It seemed in the darkness to be glowing. It came from between two trees which looked very plain and ordinary from where she was standing. Curiosity took Claire over and she decided to go around the trees to look at the other side. She found a bubble juice type substance between the two trees. (Like when you take the bubble wand fresh out of the bottle of bubble juice) Trying to take a closer look, Claire tripped over some rocks and straight between the two trees and into the bubbly substance.

Chapter 2

The tumbling through didn't take long, but when Claire opened her eyes she found the face of a girl in front of her, quite close to her own face. "Hi" said the girl in a very enthusiastic manner. "Hi" Claire answered politely. The girl stuck her hand out to Claire to help her stand up and said "My name is Kylie G. Hope and I know why you are here." "Why do you think I'm here?" Claire questioned while trying to stand up. "Well, the same reason that I'm here. You must be a wizard, because you look like a wizard, and I'm a wizard, so I know what wizards look like, and you look like one to me." Kylie said quite fast, on one breath "Actually," Claire started while looking back the way she came in.

Suddenly, music started to play and Claire thought that Kylie was going to break into song like in one of the the High School Musical movies. "Sorry, my radio is on a timer and I didn't expect to have company." Kylie said "So, where are you going?" Kylie asked "Excuse me?" Claire replied and finally looked at her surroundings. The room was painted gold and there were holes in the wall seven feet tall or so, that were black and inside each one had a blue, purple and, green spiral.

"Well you can go to the wizard world through this portal" said Kylie pointing to one of the black holes in the wall. "This one goes to the fairy world, and that one to a dragon realm." Kylie went on and on about the ten portals in the room that they were in. "and we're back to where we started." "So where are you going?" Kylie asked again. "Well Kylie, the truth is that I saw the portal, tripped, flipped, and landed in here." "I don't think I'm a wizard like you think I am." Claire confessed "Of course you are." "Only magical beings can see the portal." Kylie reassured, and guided Claire to the wizard portal "After you." Said Kylie and nudged Claire until she walked in.

Claire honestly thought that through the portal was going to be a magical and mystical world, full of color, and bubbles everywhere. Like in she had seen in a movie once. Also known as what Myra wishes of her room, but never gets because she's never cleaned a thing in her entire life. Anyways, as if going through a tunnel, there was a long narrow black hallway with purple, blue, and green lights on either side. Being pulled by a strong force, Kylie and Claire found themselves at the end of the tunnel in no time. "This is the wizard world." Kylie explained. .....To Claire, the wizard world looked only of a small town or village. It had cute little shops all down Main Street and a great castle-like school in the middle.... "I have to go, but feel free to look around." "If you need me, just follow the trees." Kylie said as she went back through the portal.

  Claire walked ahead, through the woods and to the village market. She looked inside each and every store window and found many people getting ready for their 2nd semester of school. Claire also found the most unusual animals in the pet shop. She peered at the flying pigs, six-legged cats, and three-eyed toads as she past and walked on to the next store. Looking through the book store window, Claire saw a girl with a giant stack of books in her hands and a cauldron on top.

Like in every story there must be a bad guy. For Peter Pan it was Captain Hook, For Claire it was Serena and Myra. For the wizard world it was a group of wizards who were bullies with a desire of control over the world. Inside the store was the group of bullies that everyone feared. To make matters worse, they had just tripped the girl with the stack of books, making everything fall, including the girl. Claire was not someone known for courage, but it took her over. Claire rushed inside to help the girl while the bullies just laughed.

"Why are you helping me?" Asked the fallen girl "Why wouldn't I?" Answered Claire "Nobody has ever tried to clean up the Chimeras' mess in their presence." The girl pronounced "Aren't Chimeras a hybrid of a lion, a goat, and a snake that was first seen by the Greek?" Claire implied "Yes, that is just their nickname; it is meant to strike fear into anyone who hears it." The girl reassured and finally stood up with her books and cauldron. "My name is Bella." Said the girl "Claire" Claire responded "Thanks for helping me with my books." Said Bella "No problem." Claire counterclaimed as the two girls departed the book store. "So, are you going to Merlin's Academy?" Bella inquired "Well, I just got here and I'm not really set up for anything permanent." Claire stated and headed off towards the woods.

Chapter 3

Claire followed the trees and found the portal, just as Kylie had said. She walked briskly through the portal and back into the golden room. When Claire got to the golden room she saw Kylie ordering something from an elf. "Fifteen boxes of caramel apples and I think that's it." Claire heard Kylie say to the elf. "Alright" replied the elf with a squeaky voice. With one snap, and a swirl of powdered sugar, the elf was gone. Kylie looked over at Claire and found her with an astonished look on her face. Kylie explained about the elf baker, the swirl of powdered sugar, and what she was doing.

"So, Claire are you going to sign up for Merlin's Academy?" Kylie asked; changing the subject. "I don't think I can." Claire said with doubt. "Of course you can, sign-ups are in the lobby of the school." Kylie replied as if Claire had just said a dumb statement. "No, that's not what I meant." "I meant to say that I have to go to human school, do my homework, do Myra's homework, and plus I have a big project due."

Claire exclaimed. "Then why are you worried?" Kylie asked, forgetting that Claire had never gone through a portal before. "I've been here for hours and my relatives will be home any minute." Claire exclaimed looking at her watch. "I have to go!" Said Claire as she ran for the portal she thought would lead her home.

Claire went through a portal and suddenly found a humongous, bright blue, dragon right in front of her. A young man that was no more than 12, about her age, was next to the dragon. He seemed to be grooming it and the dragon responded well to him. The boy looked over to see what the dragon was staring at and sniffing. "Uh, can I help you miss?" He said to Claire. "No, but this dragon is magnificent." Claire replied "My name is Jake." The young man said. "Claire" Claire responded "what's its name?" Claire asked "Excuse me?" asked Jake "The dragon, I meant" said Claire "Her name is Genevieve." Answered Jake "I'm so sorry to barge in, but I must be going." Said Claire and then she walked back through the portal to the golden room. "That's the portal to the Dragon Realm" Kylie said with a little chuckle. "You think?" Claire said with sarcasm. "Here." Kylie said as she directed Claire to the correct portal "Thanks." Claire said and walked through the giant, swirling black hole that she knew would take her home.

After Claire went through the portal, she rushed home to see if her relatives were home. "Myra, I'm home" Claire shouted, Claire didn't need to shout, Myra was still on the phone NOT LISTENING. Claire went to Myra's room to see if anything had changed since she had left. "Hey Myra" said Claire "Shhhhhhh" answered Myra "the phone is still ringing and Abbie will not pick up her phone." Myra exclaimed "Abbie hasn't picked up the phone for 3 hours?" Claire thought out loud "No, three minutes." "Where has your head been?" Myra insulted. Claire went to her room after Myra's insults. Claire wasn't mad or upset about what Myra said; she just needed to start on her project.

Christmas came in no time and every day before then Claire brought lunch to Jake and helped with the dragons. Jake showed Claire how to groom, feed, and the training process that all of the dragons go through before being used for work. Claire and Jake spent every afternoon together, so naturally they became pretty good friends by Christmas Day. For Christmas Claire got a laptop and a chemistry set and Myra got money to go shopping for stuff she didn't need. That day Claire went back to the golden room and found Kylie talking to a police/ secret security wizard. The security wizard left and Kylie turned to Claire.

"The Chimeras let the dragons out of the stables in the Dragon Realm." "There are not enough Dragon Tamers and no wizards know how to calm down dragons" she said with doubt. "Here" Claire said to Kylie, giving her a wrapped box. Claire then ran towards the Dragon Realm. During the week, Jake had shown Claire how he trained the dragons to come at a call, each call was different, but all dragons came to play with their dog friends. She ran through the portal and straight to the wild stable. Claire swung the stable door open, letting all of the dogs out, and then ran straight for the fields. The barking of the pups attracted dragons. The dragons dived for the ground to play. As they were distracted by the dogs, each one was caught and put back into the stables. "Thanks for helping." said Jake "No problem." Claire said in reply. "Have this; I made it last night" said Claire and then ran off before Jake could say thank you.

School came back around and Claire was still invisible. "The projects are due this Friday students, don't forget." Mrs. Jackson said and looked directly at Serena who was filing her nails. Nothing changed at home either; Claire did Myra's homework, Myra complained that she needed more stuff and more money, and Claire was still a nobody.

Most people would think that Claire would get some credit for saving the Dragon realm, but still the only people who would talk to her around the portals were Kylie, Bella, and Jake.

That Saturday, the wizard world felt abandoned and vacant. Claire and Bella where at the wizard world coffee and ice cream shop just talking and eating some breakfast. "Guess what?" Bella exclaimed in awe. As scared of the possible answer as Claire felt, she replied like anyone else...."What?"

Bella said this with lots of excitement "I signed you up for Merlin's Academy!" She enthusiastically said. Claire didn't speak for a mere 30 seconds, because she was so shocked.

Chapter 4

"Aren't you happy?" Bella asked and like the beginning of an old western gun fight, the Chimera's walked in. As a wolf pack, the group walked up to Claire and Bella's table. "You Claire?" The leader of the Chimera's team, Matt, asked them. "Why, yes she is." Bella said with pride to the two girls and three boys that made up the Chimeras. "So she's the one who calmed down the dragons?" One of the girls questioned. "She's so wimpy" agreed the other girl. Claire was too nice to say anything mean, and simply said "uh... Thanks?" The last two boys said this as if they had practiced "One, that was an insult." "And two, we're watching you from now on." Finally after literally watching them for about 20 seconds, they left. "You showed them!" Bella eagerly told Claire. "I didn't do anything! And I'm going to have to get back to you on the Academy thing." Claire said and with that they left the coffee shop and Claire went home.

"Claire!" "Claire!" "I've been calling you for two whole minutes!" Myra screamed. The only thing going through Claire's mind, right then was Oh, No. When they finally found each other in the kitchen, Myra almost blew her top. "I've been calling you for at least five minutes!" Myra exclaimed in an irritated manner Claire, with many years of experience, calmly asked "what did you so desperately need?" "Oh Claire, silly Claire, my room's a pit, be a doll and go fix that for me?" Myra said with the most annoying attitude and fake puppy eyes.

Claire of course did as she was told, not because of Myra's annoying tone and puppy eyes, but because of the wrath of her aunt and uncle. Last time she stood up to Myra, her uncle locked her in her room for a week. Noon finally came and at just the right time. Claire finished cleaning Myra's room and wasted no time making lunch for her and Jake. Right then, as everything was going well, Claire's aunt walked in. "Claire, stop what you're doing and start making the side salad." She said "Why?" Claire asked, as surprised as anyone. "Because the Winchesters are coming over for dinner tonight." Claire's aunt said in her nicest way possible. The first thing that came to Claire's mind was Serena. The thought of what Serena might do or say spun in her mind all throughout the making of dinner.

"Ding, Dong!" The doorbell rang. Myra, in a very pretty dress, heard the bell and answered the door right away. Claire on the other hand, heard the bell and plastered on her annoyed but still happy face. Finally dinner was served and Claire was the "restaurant staff", she was the server, busboy, and co-chef. "Claire!" said Serena in a kind but deceiving tone. "How may I be of Service?" Claire asked, like a professional waiter. "I'm parched, would you mind getting me some juice?" Serena asked, still sounding like she was up to something. Claire left with a fake smile on her face and came back with the juice. "YAWN! I am so tired." Serena exclaimed, and while she did, she put both of her hands in an upward motion. In doing so, she hit the juice right up into Claire's face and it splattered all over her. Claire, again with many years of experience, apologized to Serena and cleaned up the mess. Dessert that night was eaten out on the patio.

That Monday Claire went to school as usual, and noticed that everyone was laughing at her.

Chapter 5

It turns out, last Saturday when Claire was covered in juice, Serena just had to take a picture and send it to everyone in the entire school. Not that anyone actually cared for Claire "the person" they just love to have a good laugh and make fun of the person they were laughing at. Their jokes weren't even clever, but they didn't cease to exist when Claire got home. Myra was laughing nonstop by the time Claire reached the house. Saying things like "you looked so pathetic." and "that juice really compliments your outfit." She went on and on, making fun of Claire and laughing, right up until they had to go to bed. Like new and viral songs, the people at Claire's school could not seem to forget that picture.

At this same time, the Chimeras were scheming to tear away at Claire's hopes and dreams. Their plan needed brains and pretty good acting skills, which would be easy for them if more than just one of them had the brain.

To get away from the laughing and teasing, Claire decided to go to school the next morning before school started. Going to Merlin's Academy first and her human school after. You're finally here!" Exclaimed Bella. "Where's your stuff?" She asked. "I didn't know what to bring, so." Claire confessed. "Don't worry; we still have an hour before orientations for new students." "Let's go see Kylie and get the list of supplies that you need for school. Bella explained, and with that they went off to see Kylie.

"Hey guys!" Welcomed Kylie. "I heard the news and I'm super excited!" She exclaimed. "We better go shopping right away." Off they went, first to the book nook, then to the potions shop, and finally ended up at Greyson's wand shop. "How may I help you young ladies?" Greyson directed at Claire, Bella, and Kylie. Right as he did, the most handsome jock walked straight through the door and past the girls. Honestly, Claire didn't think he was the "super rare, amazingly handsome jock" everyone thought he was. Claire had never seen him play, but nobody could be as dramatically perfect as any girl in the wizard world described him to be.

He walked past the three girls, even without a glance, two out of the three of the girls melted like hot butter. In Claire's mind, if he had said a word, even a simple "hey" or "what's up?" Bella and Kylie probably would have fainted. When the jock left, Greyson and the girls got right down to business. He set Claire up with a Dragon heart string and Unicorn hair, eleven inch wand. "I think you're all set for school." Kylie said with happiness for Claire, but a longing to continue shopping. Kylie had to go back to managing the portals, so she skipped to the trees and glided through the portal. Meanwhile Bella and Claire scurried off to Merlin's Academy, to start Claire's first day.

"You're going to love it here." Bella exclaimed as they casually walked into a large crowd of students. "Welcome." Said a lady with a magnificent sapphire blue robe. "That's Miss.Tara, she is the counselor for cabin six." explained Bella. "Now I hope you all had a wonderful Christmas, and we are so glad you're back." Miss.Tara said in a convincing tone. Then she dismissed everyone to their cabins. As you could have figured Claire wasn't assigned to a cabin. Suddenly Bella bolted off to the main building which looked to be made of silver and gold with 10 different colored gemstones above the entryway. Claire of course ran after her just wondering what Bella was going to do. "Headmaster, headmaster!" Bella called. Claire finally found Bella in front of a man who must have been the headmaster, but was too young to be Merlin, yet too old to be anybody else Claire knew of. "Headmaster, this is Claire, she just got here and needs to be assigned to a cabin." Bella said politely.

"You must be Claire." The man stated. "Yeah, actually." Claire mumbled. "Welcome to Merlin's Academy." He said, very pleased with the school. "I'll have my apprentice set you up with a cabin." The headmaster told them as he nudged a teenage boy closer to them. "My name is Mason." He introduced. "Claire, it looks like we have one spot left, so you'll be in cabin six." Happily, Claire and Bella thanked Mason and walked out. The 10 cabins were in a "u" shape and each one had a different colored gemstone above the entrance, like on the office building. Claire's cabin had an Aquamarine gem above the door and Bella's had an Amethyst above hers. "Sorry to say, but I'm in cabin eight, so we won't be around each other as much as we could have if we were in the same cabin." They nervously walked to cabin six, said bye to each other and went their separate ways. For some odd reason fearing what might be behind the cabin six door, Claire slowly walked into a gigantic trap.

Chapter 6

Right as Claire opened the door a large-sized bucket of slime fell all over her. This school was intentionally meant for wizards and witches, so, anything could happen. Well, the slime wasn't just slime, but also a potion and right as the gooey substance covered her, Claire turned into a small, stout, potbelly pig. All the residents of cabin six started bursting with laughter, thinking that they had just pranked who they intentionally meant to. During all the laughter, a girl named Rachel picked up "Claire the potbellied pig" and took her over to her bunk.

Suddenly, the door swung open for morning announcements, given by none other than Miss.Tara. Miss.Tara was the one who was supposed to get slimed, right then and there, a hilarious sight, and everyone in cabin six except for Miss.Tara and Claire had jaw-dropped mouths and huge eyes. Rachel then pulled out her wand and used a reverse spell on Claire to turn her back into her old self. "Thanks" Claire said "No problem" Rachel answered "finally, another girl in the cabin." Rachel said to herself but still out loud. "What is so funny?" Miss.Tara asked politely. The whole room was quiet, as they had been for about 5 minutes. 5 minutes is the max for cabin six to be quiet. After those 5 minutes were up chatter started up in every corner. "Miss.Tara!" Rachel exclaimed "Claire is a new student and was put in our cabin." She concluded "Claire, darling." "Welcome to cabin six." Miss.Tara said kindly. "Beware of these delinquents they can get in all kinds of trouble." she added. Rachel then reentered the conversation "12 boys and now 2 girls here, I am so happy you came." She said.

That night in the wizard world after Claire had left to go to human school; The Chimeras snuck out of their cabin and met each other outside of the main building. "That Claire is here?" one girl asked in surprise "This isn't going to be a good year for her, at least with us around." One of the boys added. "We need to take something away from her that she couldn't live without." Matt said "you mean food, water, and shelter?" Another boy asked. "No!" Matt exclaimed. "Her friends" he answered "she has friends?" The other girl asked. "She has only four friends, not many but just enough." Matt explained.

No matter what Claire did in the human world, she couldn't live being a "nobody" down. No matter what Claire did or how upbeat she was acting, nobody cared. The only time people even looked at Claire was when Serena made a fool of her. It had been a week since Claire's first day and the only friend she had gained since then was Rachel. Claire excelled in potions, but wasn't the best at spells against dark magic. Claire saw Kylie every morning; she spent all day with Bella and Rachel, and finally visited Jake every evening, at least in the wizard world.

"Ash!" Declared Mr. Williams. "Explain the use for the spell: 'exclardias pevidiamus'." he asked the handsome jock that Claire, Bella, and Kylie saw at Greyson's wand shop. "To make something paralyzed?" He guessed. "Claire" Mr. Williams announced as Claire read something out of her mythological creatures textbook. "Can you tell us what the spell, 'exclardias pevidiamus' does?" "Well, it makes the person or thing the spell was directed to explode then disintegrate into a fine dust." She answered. "Exactly Miss. Johnson." He said with a pleased tone. The hourglass at the front if the room had finally run out which meant that class was over. With that everyone packed up their stuff and went to lunch. Claire and Bella sat around a big oak tree in the middle of the pavilion along with Rachel. "So, what do you think of Ash?" Bella asked. "He's dreamy" Rachel answered. "He plays dragon ball for cabin three." Bella added. "Practice starts after school" Rachel said. The girls then gathered their empty plates and went to their next class. The end of the day finally came, and Rachel and Bella still couldn't wait to see Ash practice. Claire, Kylie, Bella, and Rachel all gathered around the oak tree after school. "I've never seen them practice before." Confessed Bella "I have, it's really cool." said Kylie "What are we waiting for then?" Claire questioned. The four girls then walked to the dragon ball field which was only a block or two down the road.

"So, what's the concept of Dragon Ball?" Claire asked "you know, because I haven't been here for very long." "Well, it's like a mixture of mortal soccer, swimming, and baseball but it includes some dragon modifications." Kylie explained. Right as the four girls got to the field, the conch shell was blown and Dragon ball practice had begun.

"Just wondering, is there any special reason we're here?" She asked "Well, Bella and Rachel think number 20 is super cute and handsome." Claire said "oh, Ash?" Kylie asked "Yeah" Claire admitted "Don't look now, but the Chimeras are out by the fire pit." Kylie warned Claire as Rachel, Bella, and Kylie watched Ash like hawks. It was kind of funny how much they obsessed over him saying things like "He's so cute!" and "I can't wait to see him at the next Dragon ball game". Mumbles and whispering came from the Chimeras. It sort of frightened Claire, wondering what they were planning on doing next. After intensely watching the practice and trying to figure out the objective of the game, Claire and her group who were intensely watching number 20, aka Ash. The

Chimeras finally got up and walked towards town, past Kylie, Bella, Claire, and Rachel. Oddly, one of the boys from the Chimeras had stayed behind to watch the end of the practice. Startling, the conch shell blew for a water break.

"So, what do you think about dragon ball?" Ash asked as he approached the girls. "It's awesome!" Rachel and Bella said in sync. "What about you, what do you think?" He asked, directing to Claire who was trying to see what the boy from the Chimera group was doing. "Claire!" Kylie nudged "Oh, sorry" Claire apologized "Ash asked you how you liked Dragon ball." Kylie explained. Kylie had to answer all of Claire's questions and Claire, Ash's because Bella and Rachel were too amazed that Ash, one of the most popular guys in school was actually talking to them.

"Right" Claire said with a little bit of embarrassment. "It's... it's great" Claire said, her voice trailing off. "Cool" Ash answered "Oh no! Look at the time, I really have to go." Claire exclaimed "Can't you at least stay until the end of practice?" Ash questioned "no, I'm sorry, I really have to go!" Claire said with urgency then ran off back to the woods and through the portals. "Is there something wrong with them?" Ash asked Kylie while looking at Bella and Rachel. She would have answered if he was anyone but Ash. She tried, but her heart melted when he spoke to her for the first time.

Chapter 7

Claire, gasping for air, ran into her relatives' house. Quickly through the back door, hoping not to disturb her aunt and uncle who were sipping coffee from their custom, initialed mugs. "Phew" Claire sighed to herself. "Claire!" Myra said in an angered tone. "Ah!" Claire screeched louder than she meant too. "Latte?" Myra asked. "Oh, it's just you" Claire said in relief "Latte?" Myra asked again this time with more annoyance." I'm so sorry, I was reading and got too caught up in my book and forgot to make your latte." Claire pleaded. Myra took this under consideration and about 5 seconds later she took her right hand and pointed towards the coffee machine at the other end of the kitchen. Finally after making Myra's Latte, breakfast, lunch, and dessert Claire got her "human" school stuff together and headed off to the bus stop. Claire went through her 2nd school day, no problem.

The odd thing about that part of the day was, everybody seemed to be staring at

Claire and talking about her behind her back. Claire knew this from many years of experience in eavesdropping. People finally had gotten over Serena's "Claire smothered in juice" picture, but no one seemed to be talking about that or about Serena at all. A first for Claire was when the boys' and Serena's tables fell silent at lunch. No gossip, no gushing, no nothing. After Claire's experience with this outrageousness, she had to know what was going on.

Her first thought was, Serena. Claire was the quietest person in class, therefore making her a bit unapproachable. Serena wasn't afraid of talking to anyone and understanding this, Claire had resorted to the last person people would think for Claire to ask, but then again, Serena was the only person in school that would talk to her. "Serena!" Claire said as she caught up to Serena heading towards the bus." What?" Serena asked. "What's going on with everyone? Nobody but the nerds were talking at lunch." Claire asked in return. "I've been wondering the exact same thing." Serena confessed. "Oh, well thanks anyways." Claire complimented and rode the bus back to her house to receive about 20 minutes of silence without Myra around.

Suddenly, Claire's 20 minutes if silence ended when Myra slammed the door behind her after walking from the bus. That's my cue, Claire thought to herself. Claire snuck out of the house without disturbing anyone which she did pretty often but occasionally was caught by Myra. Claire then went through the portal in her back yard. She went straight to the dragon realm to see Jake, as she usually did. Something unusual though was that Jake wasn't in the dragon realm at all. Claire looked everywhere and there was no sign of him.

Suddenly, a figure of some sort came running out of the portal and straight towards Claire. "Kylie?" "Claire, I've been looking all over for you." Kylie exclaimed in a hurry "what's wrong?" Claire asked "Nothing." Kylie said with no urgency what so ever. "Rachel and Bella sent me to ask you if you wanted to come to the first Dragon Ball game of the season." Kylie explained. "Oh...okay...yeah...sure" Claire answered. "Great" Kylie said as the two girls headed off the dragon ball field.

Kylie and Claire met Bella and Rachel at the field and still, Rachel, Bella, and Kylie were entranced by Ash and his buddies, but mostly Ash. Claire, on the other hand was more interested in the dragons and techniques. "Look" Claire observed out loud and pointed to the fire pit. "A Chimera in the same position and spot as when we left, but it's not the same person." She added "whatever the Chimeras are doing, I doubt that one is just here to enjoy the game." Kylie confessed "I agree." Claire added. The conch shell blew and the announcer called a quarter "Cabin three in the lead with Cabin 10 close on their tail." He announced.

"Hey guys!" Ash said happily. "Hi" Bella and Rachel said with wonder and in sync, again." How's it going?" Claire asked "Pretty good actually" Ash declared. The conch shell blew once again and as soon as it did, Ash whipped around, only to run off back to the field. "What do you think so far?" Kylie asked Claire. "Pretty cool and it looks fun." Claire replied "Do you want to try out?" Kylie asked. "I guess I could try" Claire responded "Awesome! Try outs are after the game." Kylie said with a giant grin on her face. The game soon ended and cabin three won. As soon as everyone cooled off, tryouts started." So two new people for cabin four and a girl for cabin six." the coach observed. In the process of his observation, Claire realized that she was the only girl trying out or even playing for that matter.

"Let's see how good you guys are at baseball." The coach started. The two boys from cabin four actually weren't that bad, though only one was good at hitting and the other was only good at running. Claire on the other hand was terrible at both and needed some help. "Now" the coach added "Let's see how good you are at soccer." he declared. Now, this type of soccer is not the type that humans would play; same concept but different rules. For one thing, you have wings and your flying, not to mention, the field is atop fluffy white clouds. Anyways Claire was awesome at soccer and made 5 goals 2 to 1. "Finally, let's see how good you guys are with the dragons." the coach declared. This part was the easiest for Claire, not to mention she was paired up with the dragon she saw when she and Jake first met.

"Ready?" Claire asked and as soon as she did the dragon swooped down from the soccer field and into the water. Claire and the dragon glided through the water with ease. Claire and her dragon where the first to make it past the finish line. Now the coach, who can be a bit picky at times ,but concluded with letting Claire and one out of two of the boys onto the teams. Finally, when Claire was done with tryouts, her and Kylie had a "you were awesome and you did so good" moment. Unexpectedly, Ash came over to congratulate Claire and told her to come by the field early the next morning. Claire agreed to his offer and was eager the next morning to learn some new techniques.

Chapter 8

Later that evening Claire met up with Jake after she finally found him. "Hey, you'll never guess what just happened to me." Claire said with excitement. "Let me guess. You tried out for the Dragon Ball team and made it." He depressingly said "yeah." Claire said in a quiet and shy mood. Wondering if he knew everything else or even wanted to hear it. Claire asked "Are you okay? You don't seem like yourself." "I'm fine." He insisted "But it might help if you actually visited once in a while instead of going to watch Ash play Dragon Ball." Jake declared. Claire felt offended and sick to her stomach. Claire had gone every night to visit him, but Jake was nowhere to be found. She asked everyone in that realm that knew her and might know Jake, but every time she attempted to visit, Jake was nowhere in sight.

"Fine, don't listen to what I have to say, but just to let you know, I now have no choice. I have to go to the Dragon Ball games. Claire slipped out with a lump feeling her throat.

Thoughts piled up in her head, she couldn't think and she ran through the portals sobbing.

"Nice game. Wouldn't you say so?" A shadowy figure said as it approached Jake. "Matt? What are you doing here?" Jake quickly asked "I need a favor." Matt declared "What's it for?" Jake questioned "Let's just say it includes getting revenge on Claire." Matt explained "Why do you need my help?" Jake asked "you and Claire are good friends, yes? Well I need someone she trusts to help me with this project and of course none of the girls will trust me so it's up to you Jake." Matt explained "Ok then, what do you need me to do?" Jake asked as if he were ready for battle. "Meet me at the coffee shop at five a.m. in three days. Got it?" Matt explicated. Jake wasn't exactly sure if he should trust the one who constantly leads his group to outer destruction, but his anger for Claire was too strong, and he agreed. "Got it" he declared and went back to work cleaning off the dragons from their long day of Dragon Ball.

Claire suddenly burst through the portals and back to the human world. She, with tears in her eyes, ran to the basement and locked her bedroom door. Claire didn't know what to do, she had nothing planned and knew that none if her family would care about her and her problems. All Claire could do was sleep and think about why Jake would treat her that way, which she did and in three days past she was still puzzled. Claire finally went back to the wizard world to tell Kylie what happened between her and Jake and to see if she could find anything out. They decided to meet at the coffee shop at around five a.m.

"So what exactly did he say?" Kylie asked as Claire brought their drinks to the table. "Well, he somehow knew that I had made the Dragon Ball team, he also brought up something about Ash, and then insisted that I never went to visit him like I used to before I joined the team." Claire explained "Well did you go visit him?" Kylie asked. "Of course I did, but I couldn't find him anywhere. I even asked all of the other dragon caretakers. "Claire insisted." Why don't you go talk to him?" Kylie interrogated. "I don't think he wants to talk to me right now." Claire doubted. "Well you're missing your chance" Kylie urged as she pointed to Jake and Matt walking into the coffee shop." If it helps, I'll go talk some sense into him." Kylie announced as she got out of her seat and walked over to the boys' table. "Kylie, no!" Claire exclaimed but it was already too late.

Chapter 9

All Claire could do was sit there and try to figure out what they were saying. What is worse than watching your friend talk about you to a guy that doesn't want anything to do with you? Not to mention the part about being terrible at reading lips and thinking what they're saying is something totally different and sitting there, at your table, all alone trying not to too seem embarrassed.

"What do you want?" Matt asked. "All I want is for you guys to answer some questions. Is that a bad thing?" Kylie said answering a question with her own question. "Fine" Matt scowled. "Great" Kylie cheered "But only a couple." Matt chimed in. "Ok. So first off, why are you Matt working together, Jake?" Kylie asked "he doesn't have to answer that." Matt objected." Yes he does." Kylie pronounced. Everything went silent after that and for about 20 seconds you could hear a pin drop. "Fine" Kylie said and slipped Jake a note. "What's this for?" Jake asked, but Kylie was already at her original table talking to Claire. "What's that?" Matt asked and grabbed the note from Jake. He read it then handed it back asking," are you really going to go? You can't trust them." He claimed. "Anyways, about the plan." Matt said and changed the subject.

"They wouldn't tell me anything." Kylie explained "Nothing? Well, did you hear anything when you were walking over there and back?" Claire questioned." I heard something about a plan they had." Kylie confessed "oh, ok well I think I've had enough of this. Anyways I have to go help Myra pick out a present for her friend's birthday." Claire said as she walked away from the table, trying not to draw to much attention to herself. Claire quietly managed to hear the boys say something like "Tonight, I will finally get my engines." She couldn't figure out what that meant, wizards don't use cars so why would Matt need an engine. After that, she briskly walked through the doors and back to the portals.

6:00 Claire read on the digital clock on the oven in the kitchen of her cousin's house. No one's awake yet then and I have enough time to prepare Myra's breakfast. Claire thought to herself. About an hour later, Myra walked into the kitchen with a spaghetti strap, pink and sparkly ruffle dress that in Claire's opinion should be worn at a glam and glitz pageant instead of a birthday party. "So whose birthday party are you going to?" Claire asked "Serena Winchester's" Myra admitted "what do you think you're going to get her? Claire questioned, trying to sound interested in Myra's life. Honestly, nobody even had to talk to Myra to know what she was doing that day. Let's just say, she is obsessed with social media. "That's what I have you for, duh." She implied "Actually, your mom just doesn't want me around the house today when her clients arrive" Claire confessed "Well, fine!" She irritably exclaimed.

When Myra finished her breakfast, Claire quickly grabbed her wand without Myra noticing. She wanted to make sure that she was prepared for anything out of the ordinary happened; plus, Claire couldn't take the risk of her aunt or uncle finding out that she was a wizard. "It's supposed to be super sunny today."

Myra informed "are you sure about that?" Claire asked, because right as Myra had said that, it started pouring rain. "Charles!" Myra yelled and a tall man wearing a black and white tuxedo came running in. "Bring the car around please." Myra said sweetly but shortly after screamed "and HURRY!" Typical Myra, Claire thought as Charles darted to the car and pulled it up to the front door.

"Where first?" Myra asked Claire while she slid into the sparkling white mustang with a pink stripe down the middle. "You really want my opinion?" Claire asked in surprise. Myra only had to take a brief look at Claire then quickly said "Nope! Take us to Kohl's, Charles." Shopping with Myra, I think you could guess how that went. Myra loves shopping, real shopping, online shopping and even window shopping. They didn't get Myra to Serena's house until six in the afternoon, exactly eleven hours after they left the house that morning. Serena got a sparkly tank top and jeans plus some cute shoes and a tiara from Myra. "Charles?" Claire asked from the back seat of the car. "Yes Miss Claire?" Charles answered back. "Can you please drop me off at the house now?" She politely queried "Sorry Claire but I'm not allowed to drop you off at the house until ten o'clock." He admitted.

Chapter 10

They drove aimlessly for what felt like ages, but it finally got to be ten o'clock and the rain had changed to hail. Charles and Claire finally got home right as Aunt Carissa's clients were leaving their house. They were the stereotypical snobby business people you would expect to see in a movie. They were wearing finely pressed suits that looked really expensive. As the clients walked past Claire to leave, they looked down upon her with snarls acting as if they were better and more powerful than her. Aunt Carissa walked her clients out with a huge, obviously fake grin on her face.

When she returned, she glanced over at Claire and said, "If you're hungry, you can make yourself some dinner. Don't come upstairs just to bother your uncle and I. He is still working and I will be reading a romantic comedy about a young lady and her most unexpected boyfriend" Carissa said dreaming off into space, almost forgetting that Claire was standing there. "Got it" Claire replied, and as soon as her aunt was out of sight she ran out the door and headed towards the woods.

Claire stopped about ten feet away from the portal to rest, and once again saw a florescent butterfly go about its way, from the portal to an apple tree sapling. Something important must be happening in the magic realm, Claire thought to herself. Claire briskly walked through the portal expecting to see Kylie. Sadly, Claire's wizardly friend couldn't be found anywhere around the golden room of portals and magical creatures roaming around, deciding which world to go to.

Claire's first instinct was to check the wizard world and around the cabins. To Claire's surprise, Kylie was found in some bushes behind the Dragon Ball field. "Kylie?" Claire whispered to a dark figure hiding in some shrubs. "Shhh!" Said the shadow and pulled Claire down into the bushes." What's going on?" Claire asked. "I asked Jake to meet me here. Alone, but he is not alone. He brought Matt and I'm sure all of the other Chimeras are here as well." Kylie answered "At ten o'clock at night?" Claire questioned "I didn't think anybody else would be up." Kylie explained. "What are they doing?" Claire queried. "You ask too many questions" Kylie proclaimed.

Just as she said that, Matt and Jake started plucking off the jewels that hung right above the entrance to the castle. "Those gems power the great oak. By the way, the great oak is where we hang out and eat lunch." Kylie exploited "I think they should secure it better if it's so important" Claire announced. Kylie just looked at Claire with disbelief and turned back to the boys who were halfway through collecting the ten different colored gems. Out of nowhere, the four other Chimeras came running towards Matt and Jake. It looked like one of the girls were doing most of the talking, while the other three were on the lookout making sure that no one was watching or even worse... eavesdropping.

Claire and Kylie, being so far away, couldn't quite make out what they were saying, but they did happen to catch the words: I... Trespasser...near the bushes..... About an hour later, the four Chimera's left the castle and ran into the woods.

Luckily, Jake and Matt were too focused on the group of Chimeras to take any more jewels down from the castle doorway. Sadly, as soon as the group left Jake had gone right back to work plucking off the gems one-by-one and handing them to Matt to put in a bag. Thunder rolled over the Dragon Ball field and suddenly, something tugged on Kylie's shoulder and soon enough grabbed her arm and pulled her deep into the forest behind.

Chapter 11

Kylie let out a small shriek as she was dragged through a part of the forest, until she was released and dropped to her knees right in front of Matt, Jake, and the academy's doors. At this point, Kylie and Claire were both hoping that Mason or Professor Cricket would walk straight through the doors and bust Jake and the Chimeras for stealing and vandalism. Wishing that they were in a movie, where things always end up right for the main character, nothing happened.

"What do you want?" Kylie blurted out "Kylie? You were spying on us?" Jake asked with mounds of uneasiness in his voice. "No. I was waiting for you. You were supposed to meet me here." Kylie said trying to stand up but was quickly pushed back down and her hands held directly behind her by one of the Chimeras. "So, you were waiting for me behind the bushes?" Jake queried. "Well, not exactly. I was waiting on you at the Dragon Ball field and then I saw you and Matt doing something, so I came over to just take a peek at what you guys were doing. After all of that, Cla.... I mean Matt's thoughtless minions grabbed me and brought me here." Kylie explained "I knew she wasn't alone. Jake, you watch the girl. If you want something done, you have to do it yourself." Matt said and ran off into the woods with the other Chimeras.

By this time, Claire had maneuvered herself over to the castle's front and hid behind one of the gigantic marble columns. "Are you sleep-walking? What spell did Matt use on you? Did he threaten you something?" Kylie persistently questioned. Jake just stood there starring at his shoes, over at Kylie, and then back to his shoes. "I'm not asleep, or under a spell and Matt didn't threaten me." Jake let out through halfway clenched teeth. "Then why are you guys stealing the jewels that power the whole school? Not trying to alarm you, but these gems also power the WHOLE realm." Kylie said. Jake again said nothing. Claire, listening closely to Kylie and Jake's conversation and tried to quickly and quietly move closer to them by hiding behind another pillar. "Crack!" As much as Claire tried to be quiet, about two or three steps into her new arrangement, she stepped on a twig.

Suddenly, Jake whipped around holding a twelve inch dragon scale wand and pointed it towards the doorway. "You're not a wizard, where did you get that?" Kylie interrogated "I didn't steal it if that's what you're thinking. I merely found it." He replied "Never mind that. What is the real reason you're doing this? If you're not under a spell, then why?" Kylie queried. "Because...." Instantly, Jake was cut off by the roaring of thunder, the flashes of Lightning on a dry field, and the night-watchman's dogs barking in the distance. He was slightly frightened and quickly turned around to look for anything suspicious. In one hand he held the brown satchel that carried the magical gems powerful enough to enlighten Merlin's Academy and surrounding areas. In the other, he held the wand that he had found a few hours before. Jake turned around to finish answering Kylie's question, but instead found her lying on the ground, lifeless. He then realized, when he was turning around he must've flung the wand back and casted an accidental spell to knock out the person it was cast upon. "Answer the question Jake. Why are doing this?" A voice said behind him "Claire? What are you doing? Show yourself." Jake declared. Claire then walked out from behind a white, marble column. "What do you think I'm doing? You just cast a spell on Kylie and you're not even a wizard." Claire stated. Jake had no idea what to do. He pointed his wand towards Claire, gripping the bag of jewels tightly.

Chapter 12

Claire instinctively pulled out her wand and pointed it towards Jake. "Drop the bag." Claire demanded. "Put the wand away." He countered. Claire obeyed and slid her wand down into her boot, staring intensely at Jake and his next few movements. Slowly, he started to walk towards her and as soon as he got close enough to her, he whispered something into her ear and dropped the bag of gems at her feet. He then walked back to the position he was first in and stood, staring. Claire confused at what he was doing and feeling unknowledgeable about what he had said into her ear. For she did not fully hear nor understand his words. "Jake, I don't understand why you would steal something so valuable. So, why?" Jake didn't answer.

Suddenly, he heard a rustling in the forest and acted quickly. He shot a levitating spell at the satchel of gems. As the bag began to float upwards, Claire slid her hand down into her boot and pulled out her wand. She had no idea what to do but, she shot out a spell that she thought would have stopped the jewels from flying away. "Tira De Mora!" Claire shouted as a stray of light hit the bag. Luckily, the satchel full of gems was levitating near a tree branch, because as soon as Claire had cast her spell, a small, baby Tabby cat popped out holding a small mouse in its mouth. The kitten hopped onto the tree branch safely and jumped down the tree only to land on Claire's shoulder.

Claire tried more spells, but nothing seemed to be working. Kylie was still lying on the grass, unconscious. While in the meantime, Jake was levitating the bag of gem almost out of sight. Claire decided to try one last spell as the rustling in the forest behind her grew louder. "Desaparecidos!" Claire exclaimed and pointed her wand towards the sky, where the satchel of jewels now floats. Poof! The gems disappeared in a puff of smoke. "Jake!" A voice boomed in the distance. "Claire! Why'd you do that?" Jake questioned "Matt's never going to accept me now." Jake continued. "I was only doing what was right. You, Matt, and the other Chimeras shouldn't have stolen the gems in the first place." Claire exclaimed "Jake!" Matt sounded from behind him. Jake whipped around, flinging his hand with the wand back at Claire, just as Matt and the Chimeras came into view. "Zap!" Claire instantly fell back and into a deep sleep along with her new tabby kitten and Kylie. "Nice work." Matt exclaimed as he took Jake and the other chimeras back to his cabin.

"Oink, oink, snort" sounded a blurry pink object. "What happened? Where am I?" Claire asked, squinting to see her surroundings. "Kylie?" Claire shouted. "Breakfast" Kylie whispered half-conscience. "What?" Claire questioned "breakfast.... Porkers!" Kylie exclaimed, now fully awake. "Porkers?" Claire queried. The blur of pink that Claire had seen was in fact Porkers, Kylie's flying pig, pet, and companion. "Porkers!" Kylie screeched in happiness. The winged boar ran right into her arms with excitement. "I think I saw him go this way." Someone said from a distance. "Where could it have gone?" Another person asked. As soon as they had said that, two young wizards came upon Claire and Kylie. "Kylie?" Said one of the girls who turned out to be Rachel. The other girl who happened to be Bella exclaimed "Claire, are you alright?" "We need to get them to the nurse." Rachel added. With that, Rachel and Bella took the two sore, young wizards to the nurse.

"Are you girls ok?" Mrs. Williams asked Claire and Kylie as the dragged their heavy feet through the doorway, going into the nurse's office. "Sit down" Mrs. Williams said in a soft, sweet voice. "We found them this morning, behind the Dragon Ball field." Rachel explained "What do you remember from last night?" The nurse asked Claire. "Well, Charles and I had to take Myra.... I mean, someone zapped us and then we fell unconscious." Claire answered "who's Charles?" Rachel asked "who's Myra?" Bella also questioned. "No one" Kylie chimed in before Claire could say another word. "It's an inside joke from a movie" Kylie lied

"Never mind that" said Mrs. Williams "these young ladies need some sleep" she added "how long do you think they will have to stay here?" Bella asked Mrs. Williams "hard to say" she answered, and with that Bella and

Rachel left Kylie and Claire with the nurse and a few other kids with Dragon Ball related injuries.

Chapter 13

Three days passed and Claire and Kylie were still in the hospital part if the school. They felt somewhat better and Claire's fuzzy vision had become clear again. Suddenly, they both awoke with a startling sound that filled the gym-sized room. The walls were closely lined with twin sized beds and medical equipment. The sound continued throughout the hall and was found suspicious by everyone in the school, including the headmaster, Professor Cricket. "What's happening?" Kylie asked as she fixed her position in her bed to be able to look over at the two injured boys at the other side of the room. One of them had a broken rib and the other with a fractured wrist. They both looked over at the girls with curiosity about the strange noise.

"Claire, what are you doing?" Kylie whispered "Mrs. Williams could walk in any minute. She might seem nice now, but if you get her mad, there's no telling what could happen "she added. "I'm going to find out what that noise was." Claire determinedly shot back at Kylie as she led her wobbly legs to the doorway. Suddenly, Porkers flew through the door at a raging speed and plopped directly into Kylie's bed. That traumatizing experience had made the entrance doors hit Claire so hard that she fell flat on her back. Matt walked briskly through the doorway with an adamant look on his face "where's the pig?" He called. Porkers whimpered at the sight of Matt. Jake barged in as the whimpering continued, shouting "Matt stop, this has gone too far." "Jake, what's going on?" Claire asked as he looked over at her and helped her to her feet. "Claire!" Shouted a voice from the behind them. Ash, the star Dragon Ball player held flowers in his right hand and wondering eyes, landing on none other than Jake and Claire standing face to face. Jake, noticing what Ash was doing, and simply answered Claire's question with a "nothing" and "never mind."

Claire's eyes started to burn and began to water. She then ran out of the room and directly towards the great oak, where she knew she could have some time to herself. Tears rolled down her face as she ran, for she felt like she has just lost one of the only people who didn't think of her as weird or inferior to Serena, as well as a good friend.

Rachel and Bella soon walked into the nurse's office without knowledge of what took place just a few minutes before. "What is everybody standing around for?" Rachel asked. "Yeah, why is everyone in need of a nurse right now?" Bella added. "Guys!" Kylie exclaimed, as the two girls walked curiously over to her bedside near where Ash and Jake were standing. "Is anyone going to explain?" Bella questioned. "Well, this morning we all heard a strange noise, and Claire, being the curious personality that she is, got up to go find out what was making all of the ruckus. Porkers ran in, and then Matt ran in looking for Porkers, Jake ran in looking for Matt, and then Ash came in looking for Claire." Kylie described

"But that still doesn't tell us why Claire was sprinting out of here faster than I've ever seen her go." Bella muttered under her breath. "That's where Jake comes in. He and Claire were talking right before she ran out sobbing."

Kylie explicated "Jake, do you want to add or clarify anything to the topic?" Kylie questioned "honestly, it was nothing. All I did was help her up; we didn't even say anything to each other. I really don't see why she started crying, or why girls are so fragile about their feelings." Jake announced, and as soon as he did, Kylie, Bella, and Rachel all ran outside to look for their obviously hurt and unhappy friend.

Chapter 14

Claire!" The group shouted in unison on their hunt for their missing friend. They heard nothing but their own voices and footsteps, but as they approached the great oak, they heard what sounded like someone crying. They walked around to the other side of the tree, only to find Claire with tears falling down her face and onto her kitten that was sitting on Claire's lap and pawing at the drops of salt water landing on her face. "Claire, what's wrong?" Kylie and Rachel asked in unison "Jake...I...I mean he..." Claire answered as she was soon cut off by Mason and Professor Cricket talking a few yards away.

All of the girls then looked over towards a scraggly white bearded man with eyes of emerald and his young apprentice coming in their direction. "If we don't do something about it, the tree will die along with the realm." Mason announced "you worry too much Mason, but you do have a point." He proclaimed "We need to find out who stole the gems, and... and they should be sentenced to being expelled and banned from the campus" Mason announced "I agree to a certain extent, but first we need to find out who committed the crime. Girls, do you have anything to confess?" Professor Cricket asked the girls who were now somewhat hiding behind the great oak.

The four girls walked to Professor Cricket's office, all wondering what might happen to the ones who did it and more importantly, what might happen to them. "Sit down" Professor Cricket said kindly. As the girls sat down, they all yelled "We didn't do it!" Hearing this, Mason stared at the girls as if they were in court. As Claire noticed Mason's stern look, she also noticed that the portraits of headmasters before Cricket had the exact same look and their faces as Mason. She sharply nudged Kylie in the rib cage as Professor Cricket explained to them that they needed to know who took the jewels." Ow!" Kylie screeched and looked sharply at Claire. She pointed up to the pictures that filled the circular shaped office, all staring down on them. "Wow" she exclaimed.

The chain went on until all of the girls were looking up at the headmasters from many years before. "Girls, pay attention." Said Cricket as he paused mid-sentence to see what the girls were looking at. "They're enchanted. They don't move positions, but they keep headmaster Cricket and I in line." Mason said as Professor Cricket continued his confrontation. "Just speaking theoretically, what would you do if no one confesses to stealing the gems?" Claire asked "why are you asking?" Mason questioned. Claire thought about her answer carefully. This was the first time her and the headmaster of the Merlin's Academy had been acquainted, and she didn't want to make a bad impression. "Because, if no one confesses... I will take responsibility and search for the Jewels myself." Claire committed.

Chapter 15

"Claire!?!" Said the girls together in astonishment. "You're not experienced enough as a wizard. You can't do that by yourself... I mean, this probably isn't the best time to discuss the matter." Rachel implied. "I would have to agree." Mason said "anyways, Professor has a meeting with the human specialist that study everything non magical." He added. "On that note, I will get back to you Claire. Now run along and don't speak of this to anyone." Professor Cricket explained as he led the girls to the front of the building.

"What are we going to do?" Mason questioned "If you let her go through with this, then she is going to get herself killed. And If Destiny hears of you letting a new student go on a quest for something as powerful and dangerous as the gems, you'll be out of office. He added. Professor Cricket was now standing by the unusually large window that set behind his desk starring at the girls. "Maybe I'll have someone that I know is ready for this type of journey goes with her." He simply responded as he looked over at Mason with a look as if he was devising a plan. "Me?" Mason questioned in disbelief "I can't! I'm your apprentice; I should be here with you, helping out with whatever you need. Not searching for gems that could be anywhere in the magical realm." "You said it yourself, Mason. She is going to get herself killed, and get me out of office. If the destiny spirit knows that I'm sending you with Claire, then I might have a chance of keeping a job as well as you keeping yours." Cricket answered.

"I don't think that would be a good idea, professor. I think the girls have something against me." Mason explained "why would they have something against my trusty apprentice?" "I don't know. Every time I see them, they look at me differently than they do other people." Mason replied "I'm sure you'll be fine. Now, I have to go to that Human specialist meeting. You should talk to the girls about joining Claire on her quest." The Professor said as he passed Mason to leave his cylinder shaped office.

The girls walked out to the courtyard in front of the white, marble building in which the jewels were originally stolen. "Don't you guys remember any little detail to help us find out who stole the gems?" Rachel asked. "All I remember is that Claire and I were talking behind the bushes, and then someone grabbed me from behind, pulled me through the woods, and then someone zapped me with their wand. I can't remember much of him, it's a little fuzzy. That's it." Kylie exploited "Him?" Rachel questioned "then it must have been a guy." She added "That narrows it down to about half of the magical realm's population." Bella thought.

"Claire... Do remember what the guy looked like?" She asked. Thoughts raced through Claire's mind. She remembered everything, and didn't know if she should tell her friends that Jake was the one who stole the jewels. She thought for about thirty seconds, and replied with a simple "No, I can't think of anything that Kylie didn't cover." Claire suddenly looked down at her wrist watch with panic and said "Sorry guys I have to get home before it gets too late." "Don't you mean the cabin?" Bella asked. "Uh, no... I have to go meet my cousin for a.....a birthday party." Claire replied. "Oh, ok... Well, see you tomorrow." She said as Claire turned around and walked into the forest, out of sight. "Are you thinking what I'm thinking?" Kylie asked the two others. They both nodded and walked away to their separate cabins, only to come back an hour later, with a plan.

Chapter 16

Claire walked swiftly through the portals and into the woods. She looked around and suddenly felt like a character from a horror movie. Anything could pop out of nowhere and grab her. One a.m. she thought. A day there is an hour here, so it must be one a.m. She thought and then wondered why she didn't feel tired like any normal person would at a time like this, as she cautiously crept back to her relatives' mansion Then again she wasn't any 'normal' person

"Claire. I need to speak with you." Said a mysterious and startling voice behind her. "Mason? What are you doing here? In the human world?" she asked as Professor Cricket's apprentice appeared from behind her. "I have to come with you. On the quest I mean." He revealed. "I'll be fine, but thanks Mason." Claire said taking a few steps towards the house. "You don't understand. Bad things are out there, and you can't fight them alone." He told her. "Thanks for the offer, but I think I can take care of myself." Claire called back as she walked away.

Being about five feet away from the back door that lead to the basement, Claire's stomach started to rumble and growl. "I forgot breakfast, didn't I?" She asked herself out loud, and spoke surprisingly louder than intended. Instead of walking forward into the basement, Claire proceeded towards the front door. If I go through the front door, I will have less of a chance to wake Aunt Carissa and Uncle Peter. She thought. Claire then, creaked the door open to reveal a beautiful entrance hall leading to the living room and kitchen. She past the two spiral staircases and found her way into the kitchen. Please let my raspberry tart still be here, Claire thought as she opened the stainless steel refrigerator doors. "Nothing. I live in a mansion and still can't get a raspberry tart." Claire muttered under her breath "I'll go to the bakery later before Myra gets home" she planned as she grabbed out a slice of cold pizza and took it to her room.

"Now what am I going to do?" Claire questioned as she entered the basement. I could have said nothing, I would have felt guilty, but I could have said nothing and not be entitled to my word about retrieving the gems. She thought. Ideas flooded her mind as she lay on her bed attempting to sleep.

Suddenly, Claire awoke from a deep sleep. She sat up and thought about her night before, just as her stomach reminded her of what she wanted to do that morning. She slowly got dressed and hoped that her aunt and uncle weren't awake yet. Not that they would care if Claire was to go to the local bakery, but she had to be cautious. If Professor Cricket was to have her quest to find the gems, she had to be prepared and full of energy. She then looked around her room and grabbed a few dollars to take with her to town. The bakery was a few blocks away and all Claire could think about, besides her hunger, was what went on the night before in the wizard world. About Matt and Jake and what he might have whispered in her ear. Claire's thoughts momentarily stopped her from going to the bakery, but she assured herself and headed on her way into the darkness of merely a half an hour before dawn.

Chapter 17

She walked down the quiet, suddenly ghost town like street. In the darkness, Claire could only make out figures a few feet in front of her. The only lights in sight came from the street lamps towering above her. It was so eerily silent that the only sounds that could be heard were her own footsteps and a distant owl's call. She felt unsure and uneasy as she stepped forward into the mysterious darkness. Putting aside her thoughts, Claire pressed on, barely being able to see in the dim light.

Thoughts flew through Claire's mind like the owl she seemed to keep hearing in the distance, and no matter how much she tried, she couldn't fully discard her thoughts. She wondered how long it would be until she saw Jake again. She had the idea to be the bigger person and apologize for whatever he thought she had done to make him angry with her, but she discarded it with the realization of her not doing anything wrong. She still felt bad for him, though. Claire didn't think she could live with the fact that someone else was suffering for something that she had done, not that she would ever purposely try to cause massive destruction to the entire world. She also thought about how much boys confuse her. Why would anyone find pleasure in causing havoc throughout a place, for example, Matt? Or why a person would steal such a prized artifact for non-other than pride. "And people say it's the girls that are puzzling" Claire would say to herself to allow her to be happier when she didn't quite understand something that happened which was the effect of someone of the male gender.

She stopped in her tracks and suddenly, a cold wind swept by her as she past the park that was set across the street from a cemetery. Instantly, a hand popped out from the bushes next to her. It grabbed her leg and pulled her thorough the foliage into the park property. Claire let out a small shriek from being surprised by this attack. She landed in a sitting position on the other side of the hedge from the spot where she had been standing.

Claire struggled to speak or make any movements, for she was held with her hands behind her back and the kidnapper's other hand over her mouth. She had no way to call or signal for help. Claire was tempted to pull out her wand, but that may expose the entire magical realm. "Let me go!" Claire screamed, muffled by the hand of her thief. She had to think fast, and she had seen enough movies to know the easiest way out of her situation.

"Ow! You bit me!" Yelled the kidnapper as he jerked his hand from Claire's mouth. She sat to face him and squinted in the darkness trying to figure out who had taken her. The person looked tall, but had a dark mask covering his face. He was wearing dark clothes and had an unusually familiar sounding voice. "Who are you?" she questioned. "Um..." the boy stuttered as Claire lifted her hand to pull off his mask. Instinctively, the boy slapped Claire's hand away. "Well, if you're not going to tell me who you are, then at least tell me why you kidnapped me." She suggested.

"I was persuaded by them." he countered. "Them?" Claire queried. "You know

Matt and the others." he told her, with a look as if she should have known what was happening and who he was. "Jake?" Claire said in surprise as she watched him slowly peel his mask back off his face. They both stared at each other for a few moments, until a loud roar was heard behind them. "Twyla." Claire gasped as she arose from her spot and walked over towards a great ice dragon. Quickly, Jake grabbed Claire's wrist and held her back from leaving. "Why did you take the blame when you knew it was me?" He asked. "How did you know?" She asked in wonder.

Chapter 18

"Kylie" he muttered under his breath. "I guess she didn't realize what you were doing." He added. "She doesn't remember." Claire comprehended. "You knocked her out twice. Why would she remember?" She thought out loud. They stood there silent for a moment, Claire's wrist was still being held by Jake. It was as if the world had stopped until Twyla let out a howl so loud that it could be heard from the moon. "I have to go." Jake said. "Come back with me." "I…I can't." She replied. "I have to prepare to journey for the gems you and Matt stole." "Why don't you just, not look for them? Come back with me and you won't have to." He pleaded "Cricket wouldn't punish you if he thought you were working with the Dragons." He added "I have to." She answered "the whole realm would be in danger if I didn't." And with that, Claire turned around and headed for the bakery.

"How can I convince her not to go?" Jake questioned towards Twyla. "She is going to get herself killed." He added as he mounted the large ice beast. Twyla swooped up with one big movement and was off into the starry sky.

Claire looked overhead and stopped to see Jake and Twyla flying directly beneath the clouds before soaring higher. Why would he try to get me not to find the jewels and save the realm? Claire thought as she proceeded on her way. "Hello, Claire!" Said a familiar voice. "Your usual I'm guessing" said Grace. Grace was a tall brunette that was a few years older than Claire, and had worked at the bakery for about a year. Every day for a few months Claire had worked after school at the bakery to make some extra cash. During that time, her and Grace had become quite close and they knew exactly what pastry the other liked or disliked most.

"Any special plans for today? Or possibly any excuses to why you are here so early?" She asked. "Charles and I have to go pick up Myra in about an hour, and after that I will be doing…stuff." She responded. "Stuff?" she questioned "uh… yeah, stuff" "Alright then. Here is your raspberry tart." "Thanks Grace. See you later!" Claire called back as she gave Grace the money, took her newly bought pastry, and headed down the road back to her relatives' mansion.

"Whoa!" Claire screeched as she felt a warm furry tail leaning up against her leg. Surprised, Claire jumped back and looked down at her feet. "Lilly!" she said in astonishment as she picked up her kitten. The young Tabby cat purred as Claire stroked her back and upper neck. What are you doing here? Claire thought she might say. Before she could say a word, a small voice popped into her head saying, I followed you here, and I may or may not be the reason that Twyla was roaring. "Did you just telepathically speak to me?" Claire asked her little companion. The Kitten didn't say anything, nor did she telepathically communicate. Lilly simply looked up at Claire and nodded her tiny head in a motion representing a yes. Claire was dumfounded by her discovery, and spoke to Lilly telepathically all the way back home.

Chapter 19

As soon as she got home, she laid on her bed with her breakfast in one hand and her cat on her chest. Claire stared at her ceiling eating her raspberry tart. Thoughts flew around her brain as she wondered what the quest would be like, when she was so close to finding all of the gems and saving the magical realm. She wondered what it might be like if she came back a failure, without finding and receiving all of the ten gems. If this is what Matt was like normally, or if this is as bad as he is going to get. What would the corrupted Jake be like? Could he be any worse than Matt? Having no clue of what might happen to her, nor any idea how she was going to do this or where to start her search, Claire drifted into a deep sleep.

"Stop! Stop! You can't do this to me!" Claire screamed, running for her life. Claire soon came upon a clearing where she found, she was all alone. She gasped for air as she stood in the middle of a huge field. "Hello?" Claire asked to the world. She squinted through lines of blueberry bushes, attempting to find someone. Astoundingly, a blurry figure appeared in the distance, as she ducked down beneath an area of foliage. As far as Claire could see, the one figure she saw had turned into two. Both of the figures came deliberately closer and closer, until she could almost make out their faces. "Matt? Jake?" She questioned as the two figures pulled out their wands. "She's a traitor. Remember that." Matt spoke to Jake. "Wait!" Claire screeched as Jake and Matt both looked straight at her and zapped her once each. Claire was almost positive that she had blacked out, but the last thing she saw before nothingness: the sad and possibly regretful face of Jake, her once beloved friend, who didn't care how inferior to Serena she was.

    Claire awoke with a start. Whoa! What a weird dream she thought to herself. Claire sat up in bed with Lilly cuddled up next to her. She tried to use her telepathy to communicate with her cat once again to be sure that talking to Lilly and the kitten responding wasn't just part of her dream. Are you ready to go quest for ten magical gems? Claire thought, trying to telepathically communicate with the young kitten. Yes! The cat screamed with excitement in Claire's mind. "You really can talk." Claire realized in astonishment. Of course. Lilly answered. We established this last night, when we were walking back from the bakery and the park. Claire stared down at her little friend as if her situation wasn't real, and Lilly wasn't speaking English, but Claire suddenly reassured herself.

"Let's go then." Claire said out loud, not minding who might be up to here her talking. She scooped up her cat in her arms, and grabbed her brown, leather backpack that was lying next to her armoire wardrobe. In preparation for her journey, Claire had stuffed her bag full of food and other that she thought might be useful in looking for magical jewels. Claire, then slung her bag over one shoulder, and headed out the door.

Chapter 20

"Claire. Where are you going? Uncle Peter questioned as he stepped out the front door to find Claire sneaking off. "Charles left a few minutes ago, so I presume you are not going to pick up Myra." He added. "Um, no, actually I was just about to head to the school." She answered. "You don't have classes today." He recalled. "Tutoring." She replied. "As far as I'm concerned, you are supposed to be cleaning Mrs. Jackson's classroom." "Oh, you heard about that didn't you?" Claire answered, turning around to face her uncle. "Well, I was just heading to the school for cleaning and... um... tutoring" she replied, and with that was out of sight. Claire glanced back at her house as she got to the edge of the forest. Good bye for now. I'll return, I know I will. She thought.

"Claire!" Screamed a familiar voice from the other side of the portal as the young wizard was about to step through. "Rachel?" she yelled through as if the other person could hear her. Claire briskly stepped between the trees that transported her to the hall of portals. "Something has happened to Kylie!" Rachel said with great urgency as she pulled Claire across the hallway and through the wizard world entrance.

The girls ran through the portal, and past the front building of the academy. They ran until they got to the great oak. Gasping for air, the girls stopped to take a breath.. They put their weight against the base of the tree facing the Dragon Ball field. Claire squinted at the sight of the almost halfway risen sun on the other side of the field. "People." She muttered under her breath. "I see people." In fact, there were people. Claire could see three wizards coming toward her. "What are you guys doing here?" Claire asked "And, Kylie... Rachel said there was something wrong." "It was all part of my plan" she responded. "Rachel, Bella, Ash, and I are coming with you on your quest." She replied "We can't let you do this alone." Ash chimed in. "And I can't let you guys risk your lives for me." Claire countered "I have to do this alone." "But..." Bella started only to be interrupted by Professor Cricket calling for

Claire from the courtyard outside the building that previously held the magical jewels. "I've assembled your quest for the gems." He called "I have to go, but you guys can't come with me." Claire said as she walked away from her friends. "We're not letting her do this alone. Are we?" Ash openly queried. The three girls all looked at each other, and gave Ash a quick glance in response.

"Professor." Claire stated as she stepped directly in front of him. "You have exactly 365 days to find each of the ten jewels that power our great realm. It may sound like a lot, but time flies fast." Cricket answered in Claire's act of taking position to retrieve her quest. "Mason should be of great help to you on your journey." He added as he nudged Mason to step forward. "Thank you Professor, but I think I can do this on my own." Claire thought out loud as a result for his gesture. "We have currently found traces of cabin four's ruby. It leads towards the dragon realm." Mason chimed in. "Be off then." The professor said in approval. With that, Claire walked away heading towards the Dragon Realm, soon disappearing from sight.

Chapter 21

Claire treaded onward through the small grove of forest to get to the hall of portals. Once she got there, she was surprised to see Jake being the only thing standing in the way of her taking a step through the Dragon Realm portal, and completing the first part of her quest.

"Claire, what are you doing?" Jake questioned "I'm cleaning up your mess, and as a matter of fact, you're blocking the path of where I need to go." Claire replied. "You can't be serious. Professor Cricket wouldn't send you to do this alone." Jake stated in astonishment. "I persuaded him. He was going to send Mason with me, but I had him consider otherwise." She claimed. "Now please move out of my way. I must find cabin four's Ruby." "Sounds like someone's in a rush." Jake announced as Claire tried to swoop past him, and resume her path to finding all ten of the gems on time. Jake suddenly stepped in the same direction as Claire with pride. "What are you doing Jake?"

She asked "Let me come with you. You'll die on your own." He suggested "I can do this." Claire reassured. "If I can't go with you, then at least take this." Jake pleaded as he pulled a book out from behind him and held it out between the two of them. "Thank you Jake" Claire smiled as she took the book, stepped around Jake, and walked briskly through the portal that lay behind him.

In an instant flash of light, Claire had traveled from the hall of portals to the world of Dragons. With the book Jake had given her in hand, Claire walked about half the way down the hill that lead to the barn and surrounding village. She found a nice space, that she thought would be a good place to stop and strategize. Claire sat down at the base of an evergreen, and thought about how she would find a single jewel in a massive area. Where do I start? She thought to herself.

"If you're having trouble with something, I can help" an odd voice said in sympathy. Claire looked around and called for the voice. Without finding anyone around her, she thought once more of her options. As lost as she felt, Claire decided to take a break from creating a plan and opened the book. "Blank" she muttered under her breath "all of the pages are blank." Why would Jake be so eager for her to have it if it was blank? She thought to herself "If you want to know something just ask." The strange voice spoke once again. Claire scanned her surroundings looking for the body that belonged to the voice, but found nothing. She closed the book, and decided to ask a question like the voice had said. "Where is the ruby that belongs to cabin four?" She asked. As soon as she had said the last word of her question, the book she was holding seemed to come to life. It jumped out of her grasp, and floated directly in front of her. On its side, the book used its pages like a mouth, and began to speak.

"I'm sorry, but I can only tell you of things relative to the location you desire. I cannot be exact." It told her. "Alright then, is the ruby in the Dragon Realm?" She questioned "as of now, yes" the book answered "is it located somewhere in the village?" She queried for a second time. "In the tallest tower of the biggest building" it replied. The museum, Claire thought. "It's not far ahead" her voice added to her previous thought. Claire then, stood up from her position, grabbed the floating book, and raced off on the path to the village.

Chapter 22

"Hello, Miss Mae." Claire whispered to the keeper of the museum. "Good afternoon Claire." She answered back. "Are you looking for anything specific?" "Actually I need to get into the tower." Claire replied. "Why would you need to go up there?" Miss Mae questioned. Claire was now debating if she should tell the museum director about the missing gems. Not knowing if Mary Mae already knew that the jewels were missing, Claire simply told her that she needed pictures for the Merlin Academy student news. "Where's your camera?" Mary queried. Claire, thinking fast, turned her hand and pointed to her back where her leather bag was positioned. "Here are the keys." Miss Mae said as she handed the keys over to Claire. "Thank you" Claire responded as she whipped the keys out the museum director's hands and quietly ran to the stairwell.

She took the big, vintage, copper key, and slid it into the keyhole without any problems. Unfortunately, the stairwell hadn't been opened or cleaned in years, so Claire had a tough time unlocking the door. At first it wouldn't budge, then it wouldn't turn, but finally she got it opened. She creaked the door open, making sure nobody was watching, and walked into the musty area of darkness. Claire pulled out her wand and immediately it shot a bright light up the winding staircase. In its trail, the ball of light had lit each and every one of the candlesticks covered in cobwebs and dust along the walls. Their path was lit, and Claire with the book by her side, cautiously crept up the stairwell.

The spiral staircase seemed to go on for ages, but Claire eventually made it to the top. The walls at the top of the tower were open panels with balconies at every corner. The tower wasn't too big, so it wasn't hard to find the ruby. The only trouble was, with the building being so high up, birds found it easy to build a nest and attach it to the very top of the tower. The ruby was found in the nest of a golden eagle at the very tip of the tower's roof. Claire reached her arm as far as it would go, but still could not get to the ruby. A ladder, she thought.

All I need is a ladder to climb up, and grab the jewel. Claire then pulled out her wand and soon appeared a wooden ladder leading up to the nest. Being suspended in the air so high, the wind blew furiously. She rose up on the ladder in a wobbly fashion against the wind, but finally reached the eagle's dwelling.

Just as she stuck her hand out to grab the ruby, a newborn baby eaglet nibbled on the girl's hand. "Ouch!" She yelled. As the young wizard screamed in pain, the mother of the fledgling swooped by, and lifted the ruby right out of Claire's reach. It flew past the nest, and down to the dragon barn. All this work for nothing, she thought. The baby eagles were now staring at her with curiosity. Their big eyes burned Claire's heart. The eaglets were obviously very hungry, and the mother had just left them here without food. Claire had a decision to make, would she help out the babies or would she climb back down the intensely long staircase. She took a glimpse back at the little birds, which were now making what looked more like puppy eyes to her. She felt she couldn't leave them in this state, so she pulled her wand back out from her boot in which it had been sitting. She said something under her breath, and "Poof" a small pile of worms appeared in front of the four baby eaglets. They devoured it as Claire stepped back down her wooden ladder and found her way back down the incredibly large stairwell.

Chapter 23

"Thanks Miss Mae." Claire called as she approached the desk, and set down the keys. Heading out of the building, Claire pondered of where she needed to look for the magical jewel. The barn, she thought. It has to be somewhere around the barn. Claire was close to entering the barn when she peered inside to see Ash. He was brushing off one of the dragons with one hand, and seemed to be holding something shiny and sparkling red in the other.

The golden eagle Claire had just come in counter with, was perched on the ledge of the stall door that Ash was standing near. "Come on Speckles, we have to go find Claire and prove to her that I can be of use on her quest." She heard him say. Claire, listening to all of this, slowly crept away from the barn. She slid away from her position, and hid behind a nearby pine tree. She rested for a moment, but soon looked down and opened Jake's publication.

"Where is the next gem?" She asked the enchanted book. "You haven't accomplished the mission for the ruby." It responded "so I have to retrieve the ruby before you tell me where the next jewel is?" "Affirmative" Claire, obviously somewhat annoyed by what the book had told her, started to head in the direction of Ash and Speckles. Suddenly, a giant, red scaled, fire dragon swooped down low enough to scare Ash, making him jump and putting him flat on his back. With one great motion, someone or something riding upon the dragon grabbed the ruby out of Ash's exposed palm and made it a resident in their bag. "I really have no way of getting that ruby now!" Claire complained as she watched her hard work of reaching the top of the tower, and being ferociously pecked by Speckles vanish in a red streak of color.

Claire stood once more against the tree, and thought about how to react. She then stepped down to the nearby lake and sat by the shore. She turned her head down to the pond, and looked at her reflection in the water. Did she expect more? Did she think the quest was going to be easy? She didn't know. "If you can't show me where the next gem is, then is there any way you could be useful?" She asked Jake's book. "Well, I have a mirror, in which you can find anyone or anything." It answered. "Alright then, that might take my mind off things." "Just tell me who or what you want to see, and it shall be." The book instructed. "Show me cabin ten's jewel." She muttered to the book. "As you wish" it replied. Soon enough, a picture of an emerald gem lodged between a pair of stone legs appeared. Where would that be? Claire thought to herself.

Chapter 24

"Splash!" Sounded a figure off into the near distance. It caught Claire off guard, as she was so deep in thought over her quest. Claire scanned her surroundings, looking for what could have made that sound. Eventually, after looking for over 5 minutes, but locating nothing, she was forced to believe that what made that sound was a deer or other animal. Even with that in mind, Claire couldn't help but think of what made that sound could have been. "Ok," she said out loud "I have to focus on finding that jewel. I can't get distracted." She told herself before grabbing the book, and walking off into the woods behind her. Soon, Claire started feeling even more unprotected than she already was. She felt eyes following her, even if nobody was around. A few times, she had even turned in the opposite direction of her path to attempt to find a pair of eyes looking back at her.

Once again, Claire felt a small shiver down her spine, as if she felt someone spying on her. She swiftly swooped around, carefully surveying the area. "Meow." Called a voice from her backpack. "Oh, Lilly!" Claire remembered as she knelt to the ground, and sat her bag down. She opened the biggest leather pouch on her bag, and pulled out a cute little kitten. "Lilly are you okay?" She asked the tiny tabby cat. I'm fine, but would you mind not being so quick to turn around? Lilly questioned telepathically to her owner. "Oh, I'm sorry. I didn't realize that I was hurting you. She apologized. "Do you want to walk for a while?" Queried Claire to her cat. The small kitten looked up at her caretaker and nodded. Claire, then got up from her kneeling position, and walked alongside her pet.

The two of them walked for ages attempting to find the ruby and emerald jewels. As well as trying to avoid Jake, Ash, Mason, and her three best friends who desperately wanted to assist Claire on her mission. Claire found it fascinating listening to her kitten, and finding out what it was like living through the eyes of a cat. Though, wizard life was great, Claire had not yet learned how to morph, which she desperately wanted to learn, so she wasn't able see life through the eyes of another creature other than human. The girl and her cat finally made it to the hall of portals, after nearly running into Rachel, Bella, and Ash for a second time. Thankfully, Jake was nowhere to be found, which almost surprised Claire, but he had done this to her before so she was lenient to worry. "Now, Lilly, all we need to do is find where cabin ten's jewel is. As well as, possibly find who took the ruby or where it could be as of now." Claire instructed. After thinking for a bit, Lilly came up with the idea of going to the library in the middle of town in the wizard world to try and find something over stone people and gargoyles.

Chapter 25

Claire and Lilly managed to walk a great distance from the Dragon realm to the wizard world, while still trying to avoid being seen by the ones who wanted help her on her quest. The girl and her cat soon found their way to the library in the middle of the wizard world. They searched for about an hour and a half looking for things that would be useful in finding who the stone legs belonged to. Occasionally still, Claire felt as if someone or something was watching her every move. She peered back several times only to find nothing looking at her or spying. I think I found something! Lilly yelled telepathically in Claire's mind. Claire ran over to her kitten, who was looking in an extremely large textbook compared to the size of the tiny cat.

"It says here that the origin of the gargoyles is in England, but since we can't go to England anytime soon I suggest we go to a cathedral. That is the placement in England that the gargoyles were put." "I don't remember there being any cathedrals around here." Claire doubted "Yes, but while I was in your backpack I thought I saw a castle figure in the distance somewhere in the wizard world." Lilly explained. The school, Claire thought. The school almost looks like a castle or cathedral. "That must be what you saw" Claire said out loud looking over at her kitten companion. The young wizard and her cat put away the books over cathedrals, gargoyles, and distant lands that they were looking at, and met back at the table. Claire scooped up her kitten and plopped her inside her backpack. Then, Claire headed towards the door. "Town Square," she said "Town Square and then towards the school to look for the gargoyle with the gem belonging to Cabin three.

They finally reached the wizard town square, when the group of Chimeras walked out of the café. They looked somewhat less suspicious than usual, but Claire was still skeptical. She thought quickly and hid behind the wall of a nearby building, almost avoiding the eyes of the Chimeras. Sadly, one of the male members caught Claire's quick movement, and slowly walked her way. "I'll meet up with you guys at the book store." He told Matt and the others as he headed in the direction of Claire and her kitten, who was now hiding in her owner's leather backpack. Claire, now in fear of what he might do to her, ran in the other direction and into a neighboring alley.

Again, Claire's quick motions had caught the boy's eye. He started to jog as he followed Claire into the alley. Claire found a dead end at the other side of the alleyway. Luckily, there was a large building with an easily accessible fire escape. Claire looked up at the rusty ladder, turned back to find the chimera still walking her path, and then climbed the old escape ladder. Claire got about three-fourths of the way up the ladder, when she felt it shift underneath her. The Chimera had not yet reached the ladder, but he watched from beneath. Claire's escape route creaked as she tried to climb higher. She finally reached to top. She slightly gripped hold of the top section of the ladder that was connected to the roof of the building. She almost had her foot touch the roof when the ladder fell out from under her, and she dangled there like a cat in a tree. She harshly grabbed the roof to keep her up, but that made one of her hands slip even more. The Chimera beneath her just stood there watching to see if Claire would let go. Claire looked down to see this. She was disgusted at the sight of someone simply staring at her in a time of need. Claire attempted once more to get her foot above her hands to lift herself onto the roof. She accomplished getting one foot, but her hands slipped when doing the other and she fell.

Chapter 26

For once in her life, Claire was happy to see a Chimera. As Claire's hands had slipped, the boy watching her had stepped to where exactly he thought Claire would fall to. He stood there as he watched her fall, with his arms open wide. The placement of himself was so precise that Claire fell directly into his arms. Claire was unsure of what had happened to her. She momentarily forgot everything, but soon her vision became clear and she remembered what she had just gone through. The boy who saved her gently set her down, leaning her against one of the surrounding brick walls.

"Are you okay?" the boy asked "I think I'm okay, but my head is throbbing." Claire replied "Let me go get you an icepack." He said as he quickly ran out of the alley and around the corner to a nearby shop. Suddenly, Lilly slipped out of Claire's leather bag. Her bag was a few feet away and face down. "Are you okay?" she asked her owner "My vision is a little blurry and my head hurts, but they're getting better as we speak." She answered "Are you okay? You took quite a big hit." Claire questioned her young companion. The tiny kitten meowed in reply as the chimera group member came back with an ice pack for Claire. He gave her the pack and sat directly next to Claire on the side across from where her backpack and cat were sitting. Lilly came closer to Claire and laid in her lap. She also crept closer to the chimera and sniffed him as any other animal would.

"May I?" he asked directing his question towards Claire. She nodded as he picked Lilly up and put her in his arms. He pet her as he attempted to start a conversation with Claire. "So, why were you running?" he questioned. "I thought you were after me. Your groups of friends aren't exactly the kindest people to be around." Claire confessed "The other Chimeras aren't all that bad. Matt can be a pain sometimes, but it's just because his power has gone to his head." the boy replied. "Are you sure you're okay?" he queried as he lifted his hand up trying to move the hair away from Claire's face.

She flinched a little when she felt his hand on her face, but allowed him to continue. He moved the hair out of her faced and looked at her more clearly. Claire had her head down trying to avoid his eyes, but couldn't help at least looking at Lilly purring in his lap. She was cuddling up to him just as she did to Claire, and the other people that she was familiar with. Once Lilly noticed Claire watching her, she hopped out of the boy's arms and ran into Claire's. "You know, you're a lot prettier when you're not running away." He said to Claire with a soft voice. He too was watching Lilly cuddle up in Claire's lap. He watched Lilly for so long that he almost missed seeing Claire's blushing cheeks. He looked up at her face once more before Claire looked up as well.

Their eyes locked for at least twenty seconds. Claire looked deep into the chimera's eyes when she finally realized that it wasn't a Chimera at all. She knew this face too well. She suddenly recognized the one who saved her.

Chapter 27

"Jake?" Claire asked the boy sitting next to her. "You saved me." She grasped. The boy nodded as he continued to stare into her eyes. He looked at her with kind eyes, before he playfully wrapped his arm around Claire, and broke the lock between their eyes. The two sat there looking up between the buildings at the amber sky. Claire and Jake were in their own little world for so long that they didn't notice a person stalking them in the alleyway.

The person watching them from the alley entrance sulked at the sight of Claire and Jake sitting together, falling asleep in each other's arms. He looked at them with disgust. My own brother, he thought. My own brother would betray me like that. "I never would have thought." He whispered to himself.

Soon, the sun was up to end the night. Claire awoke with a start. She came to find the bump on her head that had been swollen as a bee had become smaller. But, she could have sworn she had fallen asleep next to Jake. She scanned the alley, only to find a few gold coins and an old package of gum lying on the ground. She wasn't sure if he had just gotten up and left her in the alley, although she considered what he had just done for her and thought otherwise. She soon came to the conclusion that sitting around would do her no good. Claire picked up the sleeping Lilly, put her in her bag, and started off into the town.

She looked around the corner at the old book shop and café. She didn't see any sign of human or magical life anywhere. She thought she might be dreaming, until she came across the Dragon ball field. There, she found Mason speaking with Ash. Mason quickly stared in the direction of Claire. She immediately hid behind the great oak. She didn't want anyone to see her. She still didn't know if she had fallen asleep in the alley with Jake. If she came in contact with anyone, they would most likely bombard her with questions. That is what she was afraid of.

"I can't find her anywhere." Mason complained. "I saw her yesterday, she was..."

Ash got cut off. Somewhere near the great oak, a rustling sounded. Mason and Ash quickly strode over to Claire's hiding position to look for what made the rustling noise.

Chapter 28

Claire, realizing her situation ran in the other direction. She couldn't be seen by Ash or Mason. The two boys darted to the tree. The vigorously looked around, but found a harmless looking rabbit. Claire watched from the behind one of the cabins. Suddenly, every student inside their cabin became one great mass galloping to the dragon ball field. Claire, undetected, slipped through the huge mass, and found her way to the entrance of the school. She walked through the door, and into her Defense against Dark Magic classroom.

Luckily, Mr. Williams was just getting ready for class. "Mr. Williams," Claire started "do you know of any gargoyles on the school grounds?" she continued to ask "Actually, that is our next lesson. We are learning the dangers of gargoyles." He replied. "Gargoyles are dangerous?" Claire queried "Extremely." He answered "So, it would be a bad idea to find one with a priceless jewel, and try to get it then?" She questioned "Yes." He stated as he put the last of the equipment on the desks.

Claire walked briskly out the door of the classroom with a disappointed look on her face. She had to strategize how to get the emerald from the mysterious gargoyle. Claire stood outside the classroom, and thought about how to get to the roof, where the gargoyle would be found. I have to find a stairwell, she thought. "Or I'll be climbing" Claire whispered to herself, remembering the episode with Jake and the building the previous night. If she fell from the height of the castle, she would surely die. Nothing worried Claire as much as the thought of dying. She knew she had to find another way. She ran down the hallway to the other classrooms and mysterious doors.

When she finally reached the end of the hallway, Claire had opened every door, except one. She was exhausted. She reached for the last door, but decided to sit instead. For once that day, she replayed the events that happened the evening before. Claire pulled out her wand, and was soon to cast a spell. "Penasuerta" She spoke into her wand. A beautiful luminescence sprang from the tip of Claire's wand. The memory played in front of her like a film. She saw herself climb the wall and slip. She was indeed caught by none other than Jake, her friend who didn't care how different or unpopular she was. Claire watched herself fall asleep.

She looked to the side of the movie like memory and noticed something that she hadn't seen the night it happened. A shadowy boy-like figure was watching Claire and Jake while they were asleep in each other's arms. It seemed to be staring at them, whispering to himself. The boy's silhouette started to slowly shift toward her. She soon became frightened when the memory faded, and the lights died. Claire sat at the foot of the door at the end of the hallway, searching her mind for some record of a strange silhouette. Claire, trying as she might, couldn't figure out who would be watching her and Jake, alone in an alley. What the stranger was telling himself puzzled her even more. She feared it could have been Matt or someone worse. She was fearful that the one spying on her might be plotting something against her. The thought of someone purposely attempting to terrorize her, and possibly hurting her friends worried her.

Chapter 29

Even with terrible possibilities racing through Claire's mind, she finally got the will to open the door behind her, and find the interior to be just what she was looking for. A staircase shooting up to the roof. Claire turned her head, hoping not to detect anything, and grabbed the door handle. She saw a small movement, but thought she better not investigate. She whipped her head back to the stairwell and strode onto the first step. This stairway was different than the ones Claire was used to.

This was a humongous tower, with only one carpeted step. When Claire put her weight on the carpet, it started to rattle. Then, it shot up in a spiraling motion to the top. The carpet and walls were so dusty, that it seemed to have not been used in decades. No one had used this roof entryway for centuries. The spiraling motion eventually stopped at an old cobweb filled door. The door creepily hung there. It had some steps, no more than three poking out from its holdings. If Claire were to step and fall, there would be nothing to save her. She would plummet to her death, and rot in an ancient stairwell.

Claire stuck out her foot, trying not to shake so much that she would trip and fall. She glided onto the first step with ease. Suddenly, the carpet that had led her up to the area she currently resided in now was shaking. It rattled and flew back down just as Claire's foot left it. She slightly tripped over the fact that her standing platform had just left her, but caught herself in the process. Claire reached over towards the handle of the aging door, and creaked it open. "Hello?" she questioned the open air.

No one answered, but Claire, surveying the area found faces. Faces of humans, animals, but all stone. Claire stepped through the door and into the corridor that it led to. The walkway was filled with stone figures, which all seemed to be in familiar shapes. "I think I've made it." She told herself. "Mr. Williams said gargoyles are extremely dangerous. Maybe this is what he meant." Claire looked around more, and found herself looking upon a frayed textbook, opened to the history of gargoyles. Extremely dangerous, the top of the page read. "If looked at in the gates to the soul, the one approaching would be turned to stone. Their soul taken." Claire read aloud. Claire looked around the corridor, strategizing on how to get the priceless jewel from a soul eating monster. She scanned the surround area.

"A shield!" she accidentally yelled as she stumbled upon an unusually large steel shield. It had perfect reflecting abilities, she thought as her mind turned to a Greek mythology book she had read in her English class. Perseus killed Medusa without looking her in the eyes. He used reflection, Claire recalled. She quickly grabbed for the giant shield, and held it out in front of her, before turning to the array of windows behind her. As she turned herself to the direction of the windows, she saw a red scaled body coming towards her. "Not again," she whispered to herself. Claire darted out the door at the other end of the hall. She spotted the emerald green gem in the process of running. It was in some kind of stone nest. She sprinted towards the nest. She had read that gargoyles don't move, but make terribly ear-piercing noises. Claire held the shield out in front of her, and slowly walked backwards to the gargoyle nest. Just wishing the sounds of the screeching gargoyles would stop. Suddenly, the red dragon swooped down and landed awkwardly on top of the roof, only a few yards away from where Claire was reaching back to grab the gem.

Chapter 30

Claire reached behind her, and grabbed the gem. She had successfully got one gem in the course of two days. It was all the work of the dragon and it's rider who stood before her. She dropped the jewel into her backpack, and strode over to help the poor dragon, struggling to hear anything but gargoyle. Claire reached over the dragon's neck to untie the ropes used to ride it. With one hand using the shield to block the dragon's vision, Claire grabbed the ropes to help the innocent creature to its feet. It slowly bowed to Claire in thankfulness for freeing it, and then it flew off, dangling its rider at its side. Claire quickly fell to one knee, pulled off her backpack, and grabbed Jake's book out of it. "What's the spell to fly?" she questioned it. "Valor Orbis Terium." The book spoke clearly. Claire got in a running stance and yelled "Valor Orbis Terium!" Claire glided to the side of the dragon and its hopeless rider. She briskly helped the rider to a sitting position on top of his dragon. "Ash?" Claire asked the rider, who was only half conscious. "Claire. It's not what you think. I wasn't..." Ash attempted to explain. "It looks like you were trying to get to the gem before me, as well as tried to get yourself killed." Claire countered. "Claire, just let me say something." Ash tried to convince her. "I don't want to hear from you right now. Goodbye Ash." Claire said as she flew off away from Ash and his dragon. Being the clumsy Claire that she is, she flew directly into a tree.

"Claire!" Ash yelled as he instructed his dragon to Claire's aid. To Ash's surprise someone had already beaten him to Claire dangling from a branch. Jake was climbing the tree freeing Claire, and helping her to the nurse. Claire was unconscious in Jake's arms. She hung there, not knowing just how much her friends actually cared for her. "Mrs. Williams," Jake started as he held Claire, walking into the nurse's office. "What happened?" she asked the boy. "I don't know. I was just sitting under a tree when Claire somehow fell into it. "He explicated. "Thank you, but I can take it from here." Mrs. Williams said as she took Claire from his hands, and placed her on a vacant bed.

"Claire!" yelled a familiar voice running toward them. "I found her backpack on the roof." Ash said holding out the bag. "Children I think it would be best if you left Claire to rest for a bit." The nurse said as she led the two boys out the door.

"What were you doing with Claire?" Jake questioned. "I was... She saved me" Ash admitted. "Why were you in need of saving?" he asked. "I was trying to save her, but she... she distracted me." He confessed. "You like her, don't you?"

Made in the USA
Charleston, SC
12 August 2016